FROM RUDYARD KIPLING'S

THE JUNGLE BOOK
MOWGLI'S STORY

Illustrated by **ROBERT INGPEN**
Abridged by JULIET STANLEY

PALAZZO

This abridged edition first published in 2018 by

Palazzo Editions Ltd

15 Church Road

London SW13 9HE

www.palazzoeditions.com

Illustrations © 2018 Robert Ingpen

Text abridgement © 2018 Palazzo Editions Ltd

Design and layout © 2018 Palazzo Editions Ltd

A CIP catalogue record for this book is available from the British Library.

ISBN: 978-1-78675-044-0

Printed and bound in China

Designed by Dynamo Ltd for Palazzo Editions Ltd

CONTENTS

MOWGLI'S BROTHERS

I t was seven o'clock on a very warm evening when Father Wolf woke. 'It's time to hunt again,' he said. Mother Wolf twitched one ear and replied, 'Wait, something is coming up the hill.'

The bushes rustled and suddenly a naked baby, barely able to walk, stumbled into their cave. He looked up into Father Wolf's face and laughed. Then he pushed his way between the cubs to get close to Mother Wolf.

'How little! How naked and – how brave!' she said softly.

Suddenly the moonlight was blocked out of the mouth of the cave as Shere Khan the tiger pushed his great head into the entrance.

'A man-cub went this way,' he said. 'Give it to me.'

'We don't take orders from you,' snarled Father Wolf and Shere Khan's roar filled the cave with thunder. Mother Wolf sprang forwards, her eyes like two green moons in the darkness.

'He is mine! You will not kill him. He'll live, run and hunt with the Pack! Now go!'

Shere Khan backed out of the cave, growling, and Mother Wolf threw herself down panting among the cubs.

'I will call you Mowgli! And one day you will hunt Shere Khan as he has hunted you,' she said to the boy, nuzzling him gently.

'But what will our Pack say?' asked Father Wolf.

On the night of the Pack Meeting, Father and Mother Wolf took Mowgli with their cubs to the Council Rock. Akela, the great grey Pack Leader, watched as Father Wolf placed Mowgli in the centre of the wolves with the other cubs, where he sat laughing and playing with some pebbles in the moonlight. A muffled roar came from behind the rocks. It was Shere Khan snarling, 'The cub is mine. Give him to me.'

'Who speaks for this cub?' said Akela. Baloo the bear, who taught the wolf cubs the Law of the Jungle, grunted.

'I speak for the man-cub,' he said, yawning. 'There is no harm in a man-cub. Let him run with the Pack. I will teach him myself.'

A black shadow dropped down into the circle. It was Bagheera the black panther.

Everybody knew Bagheera, and nobody liked to cross his path because he was as cunning as Tabaqui the jackal, as bold as the wild buffalo, and as dangerous as a wounded elephant. But he had a voice as soft as wild honey dripping from a tree, and fur softer than a feather.

'Akela,' he purred, 'the Law of the Jungle says that a cub's life may be bought at a price.'

'Good! Good!' said the young wolves, who were always hungry. 'Listen to Bagheera. The cub can be bought for a price. It is the Law.'

'I will give you one fat, freshly killed bull, if you will accept the man-cub into your Pack,' Bagheera continued,

Many wolf voices interrupted each other. 'Does it matter if we accept him or not?' 'He will die in the winter when it rains.' 'He will burn in the sun.' 'What harm can a naked little human do us?' 'Let him run with the Pack.' 'Where is the bull, Bagheera?' 'Let him be accepted.'

At Akela's request, all of the wolves came and looked at Mowgli one by one. He was still deeply interested in the pebbles and he did not notice when the wolves crowded around him. At last they all agreed Mowgli could join the Pack and they went down the hill to feast on the bull. Shere Khan roared in anger when Mowgli was not handed over to him.

'Roar away,' said Bagheera, under his whiskers, 'for the time will come when this man-cub will fight you and win.'

'Humans and their cubs are very wise,' said Akela. 'This man-cub may be helpful one day.' He was thinking of the time when every leader of every pack loses his strength. 'Train him well,' he said to Father Wolf.

'It is true, he may well be a great help in your time of need, for no one can hope to lead the Pack for ever,' said Bagheera.

And that is how Mowgli was given a place in the Wolf Pack with the help of Baloo and Bagheera.

Now we must skip ten or eleven years and you must imagine all the wonderful adventures that Mowgli had growing up in the Jungle with the wolf cubs. They, of course, were grown wolves almost before he was a child. Father Wolf and Baloo taught him all about the Jungle. He understood every rustle in the grass, every breath of the warm night air, every owl sound above his head, every scratch of a bat's claws as it roosted in a tree and every splash of every little fish jumping in a pool.

When Mowgli was not learning, he sat out in the sun and slept and ate and went to sleep again. When he felt dirty or hot, he swam in the forest pools. When he wanted honey, Bagheera showed him how to climb into the trees to take some from the bee hives. The panther would lie on a branch and call, 'Come along, Little Brother,' and at first Mowgli clung like a sloth to his branch, but soon enough he could fling himself through the branches as boldly as an ape.

He took his place at the Council Rock, too, when the Pack met, and he discovered that if he stared hard at any wolf, the wolf would be forced to drop his eyes, and so he used to stare for fun. At other times he would pick thorns out of his friends' paws. Nothing annoys a wolf as much as having a thorn in its paw.

By night he would go down the hillside into the fields, and look at the villagers in their huts. But he did not trust humans because Bagheera showed him a trap they had hidden so cleverly in the Jungle that he nearly walked into it.

Mowgli loved nothing better than going with Bagheera into the dark, warm heart of the forest, to sleep all through the drowsy day, and to see how Bagheera hunted at night.

'You can hunt anything in the Jungle that you are strong enough to kill,' said Bagheera, 'but for the sake of the bull that I bought you with, you must never eat any cattle. That is the Law of the Jungle.' Mowgli obeyed faithfully.

But Mowgli did not pay attention to everything he was told. Mother Wolf often explained that Shere Khan was not to be trusted and that one day Mowgli would have to fight him. A young wolf would have remembered her words, but Mowgli forgot them because he was only a boy.

As Akela grew older, Shere Khan often crossed Mowgli's path because he had made friends with the younger wolves of the Pack, who followed him for scraps. He flattered them and asked them why such fine young hunters were happy to be led by a dying wolf and a man-cub.

Bagheera, too, often warned Mowgli that Shere Khan would never give up wanting to kill him because the tiger hated all men. Mowgli would laugh and answer, 'I have the Pack, I have you, and I have Baloo. Why should I be afraid?'

They were deep in the Jungle one afternoon, and Mowgli was lying with his head on Bagheera, when the wise panther tried to make Mowgli understand again.

'Little Brother,' Bagheera began, 'how often have I told you that Shere Khan is your enemy?'

'As many times as there are nuts on that palm tree,' said Mowgli. 'Why? I am sleepy, Bagheera, and Shere Khan is all long tail and loud talk, like Mao the peacock.'

'But this is no time for sleeping, Mowgli. Baloo knows it, I know it, the Pack knows it, and even the foolish deer know it. Tabaqui the jackal has told you, too.'

'Ha! Ha!' said Mowgli. 'Tabaqui came to me not long ago with some rude talk about me being a naked man-cub and not fit to dig pig nuts. So I caught him by the tail and threw him against a palm tree to teach him better manners.'

'That was foolish, Mowgli. Tabaqui may be rude but he will always tell you about anything that affects you in the Jungle. Open your eyes, Little Brother. Shere Khan would not dare to kill you in the Jungle at the moment but this will change.'

One very warm day Bagheera said, 'Little Brother, Shere Khan has told many of the younger wolves that a man-cub has no place with the Pack, and Akela is getting very old. Soon he will not be able to be Pack Leader.'

'But I have pulled thorns from the paws of every wolf in my Pack. Surely they are my brothers!'

Bagheera stretched himself out to his full length and half shut his eyes. 'Little Brother,' said he, 'feel under my jaw.'

Mowgli put his strong hand just under Bagheera's silky chin, where his giant rolling muscles were hidden by his glossy fur, and he found a little bald spot.

'There is no one in the Jungle that knows that I, Bagheera, carry the mark of the collar, and yet, Little Brother, I was born among humans. That's why I paid the price for you when you were a little naked cub. One night I broke the lock on my cage and came back to the Jungle. And just as I returned to my Jungle, you will have to go back to humans one day. Now go and take some fire from the humans' huts in the valley. It will help you if the Pack turns on you. Men understand fire but all other creatures fear it.'

As Mowgli went down towards the village, he heard the yells of the Pack hunting.

'Akela! Akela!' howled the young wolves. 'Let Akela show his strength. Spring, Akela!'

Akela must have leapt and missed his prey, because Mowgli heard the snap of his teeth and then a yelp as he was kicked.

Mowgli did not wait to hear more. He plunged downwards through the bushes, to the stream at the bottom of the valley. From there he dashed on and the howling grew fainter as he ran into the fields.

'Bagheera spoke the truth,' he panted, as he hid beside a hut. 'Tomorrow is going to be a big day for both Akela and me.'

The next morning Mowgli returned with a pot full of glowing embers that he had taken from a cooking fire in the village. Bagheera was waiting for him.

'Akela has lost his power,' he said. 'The Pack is holding a Council meeting tonight.'

All that day Mowgli sat in the cave feeding branches into his fire pot to keep the flames going. In the evening when Tabaqui the jackal came to the cave and told him quite rudely that he was wanted at the Council Rock, Mowgli laughed until Tabaqui ran away. Then he went to the Council Rock, carrying his fire pot.

Akela lay by the side of his rock as a sign that he was no longer Pack Leader. Shere Khan walked proudly back and forth with a group of young wolves following him. Bagheera lay close to Mowgli, who had the fire pot at his feet.

When all the wolves were gathered together, Shere Khan roared, 'Give me the man-cub, or I'll never stop hunting here, and I'll never give you a single bone!'

Then more than half of the Pack yelled, 'What has a human got to do with us? Let him go back to his own place.'

'And turn all the people of the villages against us?' roared Shere Khan. 'No! Give him to me. He is a man, and none of us can look him between the eyes.'

Akela lifted his head again and said, 'The man-cub has eaten, slept and hunted with us. He has never broken the Law of the Jungle. He is our brother.'

'He is a human, a human, a human!' snarled the Pack, and they started to gather around Shere Khan, whose tail was beginning to twitch.

Mowgli stood up with the fire pot in his hands. He stretched out his arms and yawned in front of the Council to show that he was relaxed, but inside he was full of anger and sorrow. The wolves had never told him how much they hated him.

'Listen, you!' he cried. 'There is no need for all the noise you are making. You have told me so often tonight that I am a human (although I would have been a wolf with you to my dying day) that I feel your words are true. I will leave you and go to my own people – if they are my own people. The Jungle is shut to me, and I will forget your talk and your companionship. But I will not betray you as you have betrayed me. There'll be no war between any of us in the Pack, and Akela will end his days in peace!'

He kicked the fire pot with his foot, and sparks flew up.

'Brothers,' he cried, 'what has a tiger got to do with our leadership?' Then he pulled a lit branch out of his fire pot and brought it down on the tiger's head.

'Go!' he shouted at Shere Khan, swinging the branch in a wide circle, and the wolves ran howling with sparks burning their fur.

At last only Akela, Bagheera and a few faithful wolves were left at Mowgli's side. Then something began to hurt Mowgli inside, as he had never been hurt in his life before. He caught his breath and sobbed, and tears ran down his face.

'What is it? What is it?' he said. 'I do not wish to leave the Jungle, and I do not know what this is. Am I dying, Bagheera?'

'No, Little Brother. They are only human tears. Let them fall.'

'I will go to the humans now,' he said, through his tears. 'But first I must say goodbye to my mother.' And he went to the cave where he had lived with his wolf family, and he cried on his mother's coat, while the four cubs howled.

'You won't forget me?' he asked.

'Never,' said the cubs. 'Come to the foot of the hill when you are a man, and we will talk to you. And we will come into the fields to play with you at night.'

'Come back soon!' said Mother and Father Wolf. 'Because we are getting old.'

'I will,' said Mowgli, 'and when I come back it will be to lay Shere Khan's fur coat on the Council Rock. Do not forget me! Tell them in the Jungle never to forget me!'

The dawn was beginning to break as Mowgli went down the hillside alone, to meet those mysterious things that are called humans.

Song 1: Hunting Song of the Wolf Pack

As the sun was rising, I saw a deer –
Once, twice and again!
A buck raised his head from a forest stream
And a doe leapt up from a place unseen.
Hunting all alone, I watched them appear –
Once, twice and again!

As the sun was rising, I saw a deer –
Once, twice and again!
A wolf saw too, and he ran to his pack
And they sniffed the air and followed their track.
Hunting together, they pounced without fear –
Once, twice and again!

As the sun was setting, I saw a wolf –
Once, twice and again!
He moved through the Jungle and left no mark
And his moonstone eyes could see in the dark!
Late that night I heard the howl of a wolf –
Once, twice and again!

KAA'S HUNTING

This story happened before Mowgli left the Wolf Pack, when Baloo was teaching him the Law of the Jungle. As a man-cub, he had to learn a lot more than his wolf brothers. He learned how to spot a rotten branch, and how to speak politely to the wild bees. He learned what to say to Mang the bat when he disturbed him at midday, and how to warn the water snakes before he splashed into their pools.

'A man-cub must learn *all* the Law of the Jungle,' Baloo told Bagheera one day after Mowgli had grown very tired of saying things a hundred times over, and had run off in a temper. 'I'm teaching him the Master Words of the Jungle so he can ask for protection from all of the animals.'

'Well, what are they? I'm more likely to give help than ask for it,' said Bagheera, admiring his sharp talons, 'but I'd still like to know.'

'Mowgli will tell you. Come, Little Brother!'

'I'm here for Bagheera, not *you*, fat old Baloo!' said Mowgli, sliding down a tree trunk. He said the Master Words for all of the hunters, as well as the birds and the snakes. Then he jumped on to Bagheera's back, and sat making the worst faces he could think of at Baloo.

'I'll have a tribe of my own, and lead them through the branches all day long, and throw dirt at Baloo.' Mowgli laughed.

'You've been talking with the Monkey Tribe,' Baloo growled.

Mowgli looked at Bagheera to see if he was angry too. The panther's eyes were as hard as jade stones.

'When I ran away,' said Mowgli, 'the monkeys came down from the trees and took pity on me. They said I was their blood-brother, and should be their leader some day.'

'They have *no* leader,' said Bagheera. 'They lie. They have always lied.'

'They were very kind and I will play with them again,' said Mowgli.

'Listen, man-cub,' said Baloo, 'they have no Law. They pretend that they are important people, but the falling of a nut makes them laugh and they forget everything. We do not drink where the monkeys drink; we do not go where the monkeys go; we do not hunt where they hunt. They throw nuts and filth on our heads.'

What Baloo said about the monkeys was perfectly true. They didn't mix with the Jungle People, but when they found a sick animal, the monkeys would throw sticks and nuts at it. Then they would howl and shriek, and invite the Jungle People to fight them. That was why they were so pleased when Mowgli came to play with them, and they heard how angry Baloo was.

Then they thought that Mowgli would be a useful person to keep in the tribe because he could teach them new things. They had watched him from the trees and thought his games were wonderful. This time, they said, they really were going to have a leader and become the wisest people in the Jungle.

So they followed Baloo, Bagheera and Mowgli through the Jungle very quietly until it was time for their midday nap. Mowgli, who felt really ashamed of himself for playing with the monkeys, slept between the panther and the bear, making up his mind to have no more to do with the Monkey Tribe. The next thing he remembered was feeling hands on his legs and arms – and then staring down through the swaying branches of a tree as Baloo woke the Jungle with his roars and Bagheera bounded up the trunk with every tooth bared.

Two of the strongest monkeys carried Mowgli off through the treetops. Mowgli felt sick but he enjoyed the wild rush. Sometimes he could see for miles across the still, green Jungle, then leaves would lash him across the face. Crashing and whooping, the Tribe swept along the tree-roads with Mowgli as their prisoner.

At first Mowgli was afraid of being dropped, but then he began to feel angry and then he began to think. His friends were far behind. It was useless to look down for help, so he looked up and saw Chil the kite keeping watch over the Jungle. Chil saw that the monkeys were carrying something and he dropped down to find out if it was good to eat. He whistled with surprise when Mowgli gave him the kite call for help. When the branches closed over the boy, Chil kept watch.

'Follow me,' Mowgli shouted. 'Then tell Baloo and Bagheera where I am.'

'What's your name, Brother?' Chil asked.

'Mowgli!'

Chil nodded, then rose up into the blue sky, where he watched and waited.

Baloo and Bagheera soon began to realise they couldn't keep up with the monkeys. They needed a better plan.

'Kaa the snake can climb as well as the monkeys can,' said Baloo. 'He is a silent and deadly hunter. The whisper of his name makes the monkeys grow cold. Let's ask him for help.'

They found Kaa stretched out in the afternoon sun, flicking his tongue as he thought of his next meal.

'He hasn't eaten,' said Baloo, with a grunt of relief, when he saw the snake.

'What are you doing here, Baloo?' Kaa asked.

'Oh, we're just hunting,' said Baloo carelessly.

'Can I come with you?' said Kaa. 'Who are you after?'

'The monkeys,' said Baloo.

'It must be important if two hunters like you are on the trail of the monkeys,' Kaa said, as he swelled with curiosity.

'The trouble is, Kaa, those nut-stealers have stolen our man-cub, and he
is the best of man-cubs, and we love him,' said Baloo.

'And we know that, of all the Jungle People, the monkeys
fear Kaa alone,' purred Bagheera.

'Those stupid monkeys have good reason to fear
me,' said Kaa. 'But a man-cub is not safe in
their hands. They grow tired of the nuts
they pick, and throw them down. Not
even the Jungle knows what they'll
do to Mowgli. Now, where did
they go with the cub?'

'Up, up! Up, up! Look up,
Baloo of the Wolf Pack!'

Baloo looked up to see Chil the kite sweeping down towards them.

'What is it?' he asked.

'Mowgli is with the monkeys. He told
me to tell you. They've taken
him across the river to
the Monkey City.
I have told the bats
to watch through
the night. That is
my message. Good
hunting, everyone!'

32

'Good hunting and a deep sleep to you, Chil,' cried Bagheera. 'I will remember you when I next hunt, and save you some food!'

'It's nothing. He used the Master Word. I had to help him!' Chil replied, circling up towards his roost, and Baloo beamed with pride.

The Monkey Tribe was not thinking of Mowgli's friends at all. They had brought the boy to the Lost City, and were very pleased with themselves. Mowgli had never seen a city before, and although this one was almost in ruins it seemed wonderful and splendid to him.

A great roofless palace crowned the hill, and the monkeys liked to play in its gardens, where they shook the rose trees and the orange trees to see the flowers and fruit fall. Trees had grown into and out of the walls, and wild creepers hung out of the windows of the towers in bushy clumps. Cobblestones in the courtyard had been pushed up and apart by grasses and young trees. The monkeys explored all the passages and dark tunnels in the palace and hundreds of little dark rooms, but they never remembered what they had seen.

The monkeys dragged Mowgli into the ruined city late in the afternoon, and instead of going to sleep, as Mowgli would have done after a long journey, they danced about and sang stupid songs.

When Mowgli said he was hungry, twenty or thirty monkeys went off to find him nuts and fruit. Then they started fighting, and forgot to come back with the food.

'Everything Baloo said is true,' he thought. 'The monkeys have no Law, and no leaders. I have to get home.'

But when Mowgli tried to leave, the monkeys pulled him back. He could not help laughing when they began telling him how great, wise, strong and gentle they were, and how stupid he was to want to leave them.

'We are the most wonderful people in the Jungle! We all say so, so it must be true,' they shouted.

'If only that cloud moving towards the moon were big enough,' Mowgli thought, 'I could run away in the darkness.'

Bagheera and Kaa were watching the same cloud just outside the city wall. Suddenly the cloud hid the moon, and Mowgli heard Bagheera's light feet on the ground. The black panther struck out right and left at the monkeys who were sitting around Mowgli. Then he tripped and a monkey shouted, 'There is only one here! Kill him!'

A mass of monkeys closed over Bagheera, while five or six dragged Mowgli to a hole in the wall and pushed him through.

'Stay there,' shouted the monkeys, 'until we have killed your friends. We'll play with you later – if the snakes let you live.'

Seeing all the cobras surrounding him, Mowgli quickly gave the snakes' Master Word. Then he stood as quietly as he could, listening to Bagheera fighting for his life.

'Baloo must be nearby. Bagheera would not have come alone,' Mowgli thought. Then he shouted, 'Bagheera! Roll to the water tank. Get into the water!' Bagheera heard Mowgli and this gave him courage. He slowly worked his way towards the tank, and fell in.

The splash told Mowgli that Bagheera had fought his way to the tank, where the monkeys could not follow. The panther lay with his head just out of the water, gasping for breath, while the monkeys danced up and down with rage. Then he heard Baloo's rumbling war cry.

'Bagheera,' Baloo shouted, 'I'm here!' Then he disappeared under a wave of monkeys.

Kaa had only just worked his way over the wall. The noise of the fight had woken the Jungle for miles around, and in the confusion Kaa came in for the kill.

The python was everything that the monkeys feared in the Jungle and so they ran away to the walls and the roofs of the houses, and Baloo drew a deep breath of relief.

Then Kaa opened his mouth for the first time and hissed, and in the silence that followed, Mowgli heard Bagheera shaking the water off his fur.

'Get the man-cub out of that trap and let's go,' Bagheera gasped.

Kaa broke Mowgli out of his trap, and he threw himself between Baloo and Bagheera – an arm around each big neck.

'Are you hurt?' said Baloo, hugging him softly.

'I'm hungry and bruised but … oh, they've hurt you! You're bleeding!'

'It's nothing, as long as you are safe!' whimpered Baloo.

'You owe Kaa your life, Mowgli,' Bagheera said in a dry voice that Mowgli did not like.

'Thank you, Kaa. My kill will be yours if you are ever hungry,' said Mowgli.

'All thanks, Little Brother,' said Kaa, and his eyes twinkled.

The moon was sinking behind the hills, and the trembling monkeys huddled together on the walls. Kaa glided into the centre of the king's palace and brought his jaws together with a snap that made all the monkeys turn to look at him.

'Now Kaa's Hunger Dance begins. Sit still and watch,' Kaa said and he turned in a big circle, weaving his head from right to left. Then he began making loops and figures of eight with his body, and soft, oozy triangles that melted into squares and five-sided shapes, and coiled mounds, never resting, never hurrying, and never stopping his low, humming song. The night grew darker and darker, until Kaa's coils disappeared into the gloom, but they could still hear the rustle of his scales. Baloo and Bagheera stood still as stone, growling, with their neck-hair bristling, and Mowgli watched and wondered.

'Monkeys,' said Kaa's voice at last, 'can you move?'

'Not unless you tell us to, Kaa!'

'Good! Come closer.'

The monkeys swayed forwards helplessly, and Baloo and Bagheera took one stiff step forwards, too.

'Closer!' hissed Kaa, and they all moved again.

Mowgli laid his hands on Baloo and Bagheera to get them away, and the two great beasts jumped as though they had been woken from a dream.

'Keep your hand on my shoulder,' Bagheera whispered, 'or I will go back to Kaa.'

'It's only old Kaa making circles in the dust,' said Mowgli. 'Let's go!' And the three of them slipped off through a gap in the wall.

'Ugh!' said Baloo, when he stood under the trees again. 'I'll never trust Kaa again.' He shook himself all over.

'He knows more than we do,' said Bagheera, trembling. 'If I had stayed, I would have walked down his throat.'

'But I don't understand,' laughed Mowgli. 'I just saw a big snake making silly circles until it got dark.'

'Mowgli,' said Bagheera angrily, 'it's not funny. We are both badly hurt – Baloo's nose, neck and shoulders are sore because of you and my ears and sides and paws have been bitten because of you. Neither of us will be able to enjoy hunting for many days – and Kaa's Hunger Dance made us both stupid. All because you played with the Monkey Tribe.'

'It's true,' said Mowgli sadly. 'I'm a bad man-cub.'

'Jump on my back, Little Brother, and we'll go home,' said Bagheera. So, Mowgli laid his head down on Bagheera's back and slept so deeply that he did not even wake when he was put down by Mother Wolf's side in the cave.

SONG 2: ROAD SONG OF THE MONKEY TRIBE

Here we go, up into the trees,
Near to the sky, where no one sees!
Don't you envy our skillfulness?
Don't you wish you were more like us?
Wouldn't you like a tail this long?
And feet so clever and so strong?
Now you're angry, but — never mind!
This is the way of monkey-kind!

Here we sit in a branchy row,
And think of all the things we know.
We dream of jobs we want to do —
It only takes a minute, too!
Jobs which are noble, brave and good,
And done just by wishing we could.
Now we're going to … never mind!
This is the way of monkey-kind!

All the talk we have ever heard
Spoken by bat or beast or bird —
Those with skin or fur or feather —
Shout it quickly all together!
Excellent! Well done! Once again!
Now we are talking just like men.
Let's pretend we are … never mind!
This is the way of monkey-kind!

Through the trees we sweep, join us as we leap,
High up in the canopy where the wild grape swings.
By the trees that we shake and the noise that we make,
Be sure, we're going to do some brilliant things!

TIGER! TIGER!

Now we must return to the first tale. When Mowgli left the wolf's cave after the fight with the Pack at the Council Rock, he ran down past the village and kept running for nearly twenty miles, until he came to another little village with cattle and buffalo grazing nearby.

When the little boys in charge of the herds saw Mowgli, they shouted and ran away. Mowgli followed them and, when he got to the village, there were at least a hundred people waiting at the gate, who stared and talked and shouted and pointed at Mowgli.

'There's nothing to be afraid of,' said one of the men. 'Look at the marks on his arms and legs. They are wolf bites. He's a wolf-child that's run away from the Jungle.'

'Poor child!' said a woman. 'He looks a lot like the boy that was taken by the tiger.'

'He does look like my boy,' said another woman, staring at Mowgli.

'This is like when I joined the Wolf Pack!' thought Mowgli. 'Well, if I am a man, I must become one.'

The crowd parted as Mowgli followed the woman to her hut. She gave him some milk and bread, and then she put her hand on his head and looked into his eyes.

'You are very like my son, and you will be my son.'

Mowgli was uneasy. He had never been under a roof before, but he knew he could escape if he wanted to.

'What's the good of a person,' he said to himself at last, 'if they do not understand people? Now I am as silly and dumb as a man would be in the Jungle. I must learn their language.'

Mowgli had learned to copy all the sounds of the Jungle animals, so human words were easy for him. Before dark, he had learned the names of many things in the hut, but he did not want to sleep there.

As he stretched himself out in some long, clean grass at the edge of the field, a soft, grey nose poked him under the chin.

'You smell like a man already,' said his eldest wolf brother. 'Wake up, Little Brother! I have news.'

'Is everyone in the Jungle all right?' said Mowgli, hugging him.

'Shere Khan has left, but he says he's going to kill you when he returns.'

'I've made the same promise. Grey Brother, I'm tired tonight but will you come again with news?'

'Yes, but you won't forget you're a wolf, will you?' asked Grey Brother anxiously.

'Never. I'll always remember I love you and everyone in our cave, but I'll never forget that the Pack threw me out.'

'You could be thrown out of the human pack, too. I'll come back soon with more news.'

For three months after that night, Mowgli didn't leave the village. He was busy learning about humans. He had to wear clothes, which annoyed him, and learn about money and farming, which he thought were pointless.

In the Jungle, Mowgli was weak compared with the beasts, but in the village people said that he was as strong as a bull. They decided that Mowgli should start work as soon as possible.

The head of the village told Mowgli he would herd the buffaloes the next day while they grazed. This made Mowgli very happy. That night, he joined the circle of villagers that met every evening on a platform under a huge fig tree. There was a hole under the platform where a cobra lived and every night the villagers left him a little plate of milk as a sign of respect. They told wonderful stories and most of them were about the Jungle because it was so close to their homes. As they told their tales, the monkeys sat and talked in the upper branches of the great tree. Their stories were about the deer and the wild pigs that grubbed up their crops, and now and again about the tiger that carried off a man at twilight, within sight of the village gates. The most wonderful ones were told by an old hunter, and when he told them the children's eyes grew wider and wider.

Mowgli had to cover his face to hide his laughter and his shoulders shook as the hunter went from one wonderful story to another. He was explaining how the ghost of a nasty old man controlled the tiger that had carried Mowgli away.

'I know it's true,' he said, 'because the tiger limps just like the old man used to. I can see it from his tracks.'

'True, true,' said the old men, nodding.

'Rubbish!' said Mowgli. 'Everyone knows that tiger limps because he was born lame.'

The hunter was speechless with surprise for a moment. Then he replied, 'If you're so wise, Jungle brat, bring us his hide. Better still, don't interrupt when your elders are speaking.'

Mowgli stood up. 'All evening I've sat here listening,' he called back over his shoulder, 'and you've hardly said one word of truth about the Jungle.'

At dawn, Mowgli rode through the village on the back of the great herd bull, Rama. He told the village boys to graze the cattle, while he went on alone with the buffaloes. Then he drove them to the edge of the plain and went to find Grey Brother.

'I've waited here for days,' said Grey Brother. 'Why are you herding cattle?'

'I'm a village herd now,' said Mowgli. 'What's happening with Shere Khan?'

'He came back and waited for you. Then he left again.'

'Good,' said Mowgli. Then he lay down in the shade and slept while the buffaloes grazed around him. Then, one after another, they worked their way into the mud until only their noses and eyes showed above the surface, and there they lay under the hot sun like logs. One kite whistled almost out of sight overhead, and Mowgli knew that if he died, a score of hungry kites would arrive out of nowhere. The day seemed to last for ever, but then evening came, and the children called, and the buffaloes got up out of the sticky mud, and they moved across the plain back to the twinkling lights of the village.

Day after day Mowgli led the buffaloes out to their wallows. He would see Grey

Brother's back a mile and a half away across the plain (so he knew that Shere Khan had

not come back). Day after day he would lie on the grass listening to the noises around him,

and dreaming of the old days in the Jungle.

Then one day he did not see Grey Brother, and he knew Shere Khan was nearby.

Mowgli laughed and headed the buffaloes for the ravine. Grey Brother was waiting for him,

every bristle on his back lifted.

'Shere Khan has hidden for a month to throw you off your guard. He crossed the

mountains last night with Tabaqui the jackal, hot on your trail,' said the wolf, panting.

'I am not afraid of Shere Khan,' Mowgli replied, 'but Tabaqui is very cunning.'

'Don't worry,' said Grey Brother, licking his lips a little. 'I met Tabaqui at dawn. Now

he is making a nice meal for the kites, but he told me everything before I broke his back.

Shere Khan is on your trail. His plan is to wait for you at the village gate this evening. He's

hiding in the ravine at the moment.'

'Has he eaten today?' said Mowgli. The answer meant life or death to him.

'He killed a pig at dawn and he has had a big drink, too. Remember, Shere Khan could

never fast, even for the sake of revenge.'

'And he thinks that I'll wait until he has finished sleeping! These buffaloes will not

charge unless they smell him, and I cannot speak their language. Can we get behind his

trail so that they can sniff him out?'

'He swam far down the river to hide his scent,' said Grey Brother.

'Tabaqui must have told him that. He would never have thought of it by himself,' said

Mowgli. Then he stood with his finger in his mouth, thinking.

'The ravine opens out on the plain less than half a mile from here. I can take the herd

round through the Jungle to the head of the ravine and then sweep down. We must block

one end. Grey Brother, can you split the herd in two?'

'Perhaps with some help,' said Grey Brother, and suddenly a huge grey head that was very familiar to Mowgli lifted up from the long grass. Then the hot air was filled with the loneliest cry in all of the Jungle – the hunting-howl of a wolf at midday.

'Akela!' said Mowgli, clapping his hands. 'I knew you wouldn't forget me. We have work to do! We need to cut the herd in two. Can you keep the cows and calves together, and the bulls by themselves?'

The two wolves ran, weaving in between the members of the herd, who snorted and threw their heads up, and separated into two groups. The cows stood in one group with their calves in the centre. They glared and pawed, ready to charge and trample the life out of the wolves the moment they stood still. In the other group, the bulls snorted and stamped, but, although they looked more frightening, they were much less dangerous, because they had no calves to protect.

Humans could not have divided the herd so neatly and so quickly.

'Drive the bulls to the top of the ravine, Akela,' said Mowgli, climbing on to Rama's

back. 'Grey Brother, drive the cows into the bottom of the ravine.'

The angry bulls moved very fast and threw up big clouds of dust, which made the

children hurry back to the village crying that the buffaloes had gone mad and run away.

Mowgli's plan was simple. He wanted to trap Shere Khan in the ravine between the bulls

and the cows. After his big meal, Mowgli knew that Shere Khan would be unable to fight or

climb the sides of the ravine.

When the buffaloes were in position, Mowgli looked down at the sides of the ravine, and

he saw that they would be impossible for a tiger to climb. He put his hands to his mouth.

'Shere Khan,' he shouted, 'you're trapped.'

After a long time the sleepy snarl of a full-fed tiger came back.

'Who's that?' said Shere Khan.

'It's Mowgli!' The echoes jumped from rock to rock. 'Hurry the buffaloes down, Akela!'

he shouted, kicking Rama's sides. The herd paused for a second and then plunged forwards.

Then Rama smelled Shere Khan, and he bellowed the battle cry.

Hearing the thunder of hooves, Shere Khan picked himself up and lumbered down the

ravine, looking for a way to escape, but there was none. The bulls came bellowing after

him, and the cows at the bottom of the ravine answered them. Mowgli saw Shere Khan

turn back towards the bulls – he would rather face them than the cows with their calves.

Then Rama tripped, stumbled and trampled over something soft, with the bulls at his

heels. Then they all crashed into the other herd and raced out of the bottom of the ravine.

Mowgli waited until the herd began to calm down, and then he slipped off Rama's neck.

'It's all over,' he said.

Shere Khan had died beneath Rama's hooves.

The kites were coming for Shere Khan's body already.

'Brothers, that was a horrible way to die,' said Mowgli, feeling for the knife he always carried around his neck now that he lived with humans. 'But Shere Khan would never have fought fairly. It's time to take his hide to the Council Rock. We must work quickly.'

A village boy would never have dreamed of skinning a ten-foot tiger alone, but Mowgli knew better than anyone how to skin an animal. It was hard work and after an hour a hand fell on his shoulder. It was the village hunter. He had rushed out after the children had told the village about the buffalo stampede, anxious to punish Mowgli for not taking better care of the herd.

'What are you doing?' he growled. 'You can't skin a tiger! I'll do it. I can get money for this tiger hide!'

'No!' said Mowgli. 'I need the skin for my own use. Go away, old man!'

'How dare you talk to me like that! Give me the tiger, you little brat!'

'Akela,' said Mowgli, 'this old ape is bothering me.'

Suddenly the hunter found himself flat on the grass, with a grey wolf standing over him. Mowgli went on skinning Shere Khan.

'Listen,' Mowgli said, between his teeth. 'There is an old war between this tiger and me – and I have won.'

If the hunter had been ten years younger, he would have taken his chance with Akela. But a wolf that obeyed the orders of a boy, who had a private war with a man-eating tiger, was not a common animal so the hunter lay very still.

'Great king!' he said at last, in a husky whisper.

'Yes,' said Mowgli, without turning his head, chuckling a little.

'I'm an old man,' he said at last. 'I did not know you were anything more than a herd-boy. Please let me go!'

'Let him go, Akela,' said Mowgli, and the hunter hobbled back to the village as fast as
he could, looking back over his shoulder in case Mowgli changed into something terrible.

Mowgli went on with his work, but it was nearly twilight before he and the wolves had
finished removing the beautiful bright coat from Shere Khan's body.

'Now we must hide this fur and take the buffaloes home! Help me to herd them, Akela.'

They rounded up the herd in the misty twilight, and when they got near the village
Mowgli saw lights, and heard the blowing of horns and the banging of bells. Half the
village seemed to be waiting for him by the gate.

'That is because I have killed Shere Khan,' he said to himself but, as he got closer,
a shower of stones whistled past his ears, and the villagers shouted, 'Wolf's brat! Jungle-
devil! Go away!'

59

'These brothers of yours have thrown you out, like the Pack did,' said Akela.

'Again?' said Mowgli. 'Last time, it was because I was a man. Now it's because I'm a wolf. Let's go, Akela.'

The woman who had looked after Mowgli cried, 'My son! They say you can turn yourself into a beast. I do not believe it, but you must leave or they will kill you.'

'This is one of the stupid stories they tell under the big tree at dusk, village mother,' he answered. 'Goodbye!' Then the buffaloes charged through the gate, scattering the crowd, and Mowgli turned and walked away with Akela. As he looked up at the stars he felt happy.

The moon was sinking when Mowgli and the two wolves came to Mother Wolf's cave.

'The Man Pack have thrown me out, Mother,' shouted Mowgli, 'but I have Shere Khan's hide.'

Mother Wolf's eyes glowed when she saw the skin.

'I told him that you would kill him one day. Well done.'

'Yes, Little Brother, well done,' said a deep voice. 'We were lonely without you.' It was Bagheera.

They clambered up the Council Rock together, and Mowgli spread the skin out on the flat stone. Then a song came to Mowgli, and he sang it, leaping up and down on the skin, until he had no more breath left, while Grey Brother and Akela howled between the verses.

'Man Pack and Wolf Pack have thrown me out,' said Mowgli. 'Now I will hunt alone in the Jungle.'

'We will hunt with you,' said his four cub brothers. So Mowgli went away and hunted with the four cubs in the Jungle from that day on.

SONG 3: MOWGLI'S SONG

Let me sing Mowgli's song – it's all my own!
Let the Jungle hear how much I have grown.
Shere Khan said he'd kill the man-cub Mowgli!

Then he ate, drank and slept – and dreamt of me.
Shere Khan, when will you eat and drink again?
Sleep well but do not dream of killing men.

Now I'm all alone on the grazing grounds.
Grey Brother, come to me! Take leaps and bounds!
Come on, Akela! There's good hunting here.
Bring up the buffaloes – they have no fear.
Drive them here and there, as I tell you to.

Wake up, Shere Khan! Oh, I'm coming for you!
The king of the buffaloes stamps his hooves,
Shere Khan is surrounded before he moves!
What does Shere Khan do when he wants to flee?
Mang the bat hangs upside down in a tree,
The porcupine Ikki digs his way out,
And Mao the peacock flies off with a shout.

But poor old Shere Khan has nowhere to go,
As the buffaloes bring their heads down low.
Then I see him fall under Rama's feet.
Oh, he won't wake up from this final sleep!
The kites come down and they circle his head,
The black ants come up to see if he's dead.

Many creatures come to see what I've done
As I skin Shere Khan under the hot sun.
The kites are waiting to begin their feast,
And I've won so lend me your coat, old beast!
Lend me your coat so I can show my Pack.
I've made a promise to take your coat back.

With a knife, I take Shere Khan's final gift.
This is Shere Khan's heavy hide that I lift!
But the Man Pack do not like what they see,
First they shout and then they throw stones at me.
I turn and I run, I run for my life,
Holding Shere Khan's coat and my hunting knife.

Wolf brothers, run with me through the hot night,
Leave the lights of the village for moonlight.
The Man Pack didn't want me as their friend
And the Wolf Pack made me leave in the end.
Jungle and village are closed to me. Why?
Mang is half beast and half bird in the sky,
And I fly between Man and Jungle. Why?

Being in the Jungle makes my heart light
But my feelings start to struggle and fight.
I have Shere Khan's hide, but my heart is sad
Because now the village thinks that I'm bad.
Tears fall from my eyes, I laugh when they land,
I'm two Mowglis, with this knife in my hand,
My heart's full of things I don't understand.